THE PINSTRIPE
GHOST

THE PINSTRIPE
GHOST

by David A. Kelly
illustrated by Mark Meyers

A STEPPING STONE BOOK™
Random House 🏠 New York

*To my wife, Alice, who started all this by letting
our sons stay up <u>way</u> past their bedtime watching
the Boston Red Sox on TV. —D.A.K.*

*To Mom and Dad, for all the support and for letting me be crazy!
—M.M.*

*"I swing big, with everything I've got. I hit big or I miss big.
I like to live as big as I can." —Babe Ruth*

Text copyright © 2011 by David A. Kelly
Cover art and interior illustrations copyright © 2011 by Mark Meyers

Published in the United States by Random House Children's Books, a division of Random House LLC, New York, a Penguin Random House Company.

Random House and the colophon are registered trademarks and A Stepping Stone Book and the colophon are trademarks of Random House LLC. Ballpark Mysteries is a registered trademark of Upside Research, Inc.

Visit us on the Web!
SteppingStonesBooks.com
randomhouse.com/kids

Educators and librarians, for a variety of teaching tools, visit us at
RHTeachersLibrarians.com

Library of Congress Cataloging-in-Publication Data
Kelly, David A. (David Andrew)
The pinstripe ghost / by David A. Kelly ; illustrated by Mark Meyers. — 1st ed.
p. cm. — (Ballpark mysteries ; #2)
"A Stepping Stone Book."
Summary: While visiting New York's Yankee Stadium with Kate's mother, cousins Mike and Kate decide to investigate the rumor that the ghost of Babe Ruth is haunting the stadium.
ISBN 978-0-375-86704-0 (trade) — ISBN 978-0-375-96704-7 (lib. bdg.) —
ISBN 978-0-375-89817-4 (ebook)
[1. Baseball—Fiction. 2. Ghosts—Fiction. 3. Cousins—Fiction. 4. Yankee Stadium (New York, N.Y. : 2009–)—Fiction. 5. Mystery and detective stories.] I. Meyers, Mark, ill.
II. Title.
PZ7.K2936Pi 2011 [Fic]—dc22 2010016545

Printed in the United States of America
20 19

Contents

Spooky News

Mike Walsh had always wanted to visit Yankee Stadium. But now that he was there, he just wanted to leave.

"When do you think this will be over?" he asked his cousin, Kate Hopkins. The two were sitting in the back row of a press conference at the stadium. "I can't wait to try out that rooftop pool at the hotel!"

"Soon. You know my mom—super sports reporter!" Kate said. She pulled her long brown ponytail through the back of a blue Cooperstown baseball cap. "She always likes to stay until the end and get in one last question."

"Just like you," Mike teased.

Kate's mother was a reporter for the website American Sportz. She and the kids were at Yankee Stadium in New York City for a spring weekend series against the Seattle Mariners. They had driven down that morning from their home in upstate New York.

Mike pulled a well-worn baseball out of the front pouch of his sweatshirt. He tossed it from hand to hand. "When we get back to the hotel, let's see who can swim underwater the farthest!" he said.

"Sure. But don't make everything a competition," Kate said, "unless you want to keep losing!"

Mike rolled his eyes. He was good at sports. But Kate was, too. Sports were a big deal to both of their families. Kate's mom used to be a pro softball player, and her dad was a baseball scout. Mike's parents owned a sporting goods store in Cooperstown.

At the front of the room, a team official was talking about the upcoming series. The first Mariners-Yankees game was the next day.

Mike drummed his fingers on the side of his chair. He liked action more than talk, and press conferences were *all* talk and *no* action. But at least it was baseball talk.

The official finished answering a question. "That's it for today," he said. "Except for one last thing. The famous author Mr. Robert Williams will be here all weekend near the main entrance. He'll be signing copies of his new book, *Ghosts in the Ballpark: A History of Haunted Baseball Stadiums and Super-natural Superstars.*"

"What about the ghost of Babe Ruth?" Mrs. Hopkins asked. "Will he show up this weekend?"

Kate turned to Mike, her brown eyes wide. "A ghost?" she asked. "How come Mom didn't tell us about it?"

"Aunt Laura probably wanted it to be a surprise," Mike replied. Suddenly, he wasn't bored at all. "Shh. I want to hear what he says."

"Ummmm . . . I—I don't know," the man stammered. He mopped his brow and riffled through his papers. Mike thought he looked as if he was stalling for time. "Officially, there aren't any ghosts in Yankee Stadium."

"Some people are saying that the stadium is haunted," Mrs. Hopkins added, "because the original Yankee Stadium where Babe Ruth played was torn down and this new one was built."

A few of the other reporters nodded.

"I talked to some workers. They have heard strange noises," a reporter with long blond hair put in.

"Oh, noises," the official said. He waved a hand. "Yankee Stadium is big. You'll always have some funny noises here and there. But those stories about a ghost are just that—stories." He gave a nervous laugh.

"So you have no comment about Babe Ruth's ghost?" Mrs. Hopkins asked. "Or if he'll be here this weekend?"

"No," the official said. "Leave the questions about supernatural superstars to Mr. Williams. He's the expert. We'll focus on baseball."

Mike had never heard anything so cool. He leaned toward Kate. "Let's try to find the ghost!" he said.

At last the press conference was over. Kate and Mike went out to the hallway to wait for Mrs. Hopkins.

Kate stayed busy by counting in Spanish. She kept track of the numbers using her fingers. *"Uno, dos, tres, cuatro, cinco, seis, siete, ocho, nueve, diez . . ."*

Kate's father spoke Spanish and she wanted to learn. So she was teaching herself by reading books and practicing.

Five minutes went by. Kate tapped her foot. Sometimes her mom got caught up talking to other reporters. She needed Kate to remind her to move along.

"I'm going to go find my mom," Kate said to Mike. "We'll meet you here."

Kate stepped back into the pressroom. Meanwhile, Mike leaned against a soda machine and tossed his baseball back and forth. The crowd of reporters thinned out.

Whoosh!

The baseball slipped past Mike's left hand.

Clunk . . . clunk . . . clunk.

The ball bounced on the floor and rolled into the foot of a passing workman. He was wearing a blue shirt that read ACE AIR-CONDITIONING. Little white clouds and icicles circled the words. Another workman was following him.

The first workman bent down and picked up the ball. "Hey, you'd better work on your catches, Mickey Mantle!" he said. He tossed the baseball back to Mike. "You're not going to make it to the Yankees with that kind of fielding."

"Thanks," Mike said. A blush spread over his freckled face. "Sorry."

"No problem," the workman said. Mike looked more closely at him. Curly red hair poked out from under his Yankees baseball cap. He wasn't very old at all, probably a teenager.

"Come on, Sammy," the other workman

said. "We have to finish fixing that air conditioner by the end of today. Tomorrow's a game day. We won't be allowed in the stadium."

"Okay, Dad." Sammy smiled at Mike and then ran to catch up with his father.

Mike went back to tossing the ball. The hallway was quiet.

"Boo!"

Mike jumped about a foot. The baseball flew out of his hands and bounced down the hall again. Kate and Mrs. Hopkins laughed as Mike scrambled after it.

"Thinking about ghosts?" asked Kate.

"No, just one ghost," Mike said. "Babe Ruth's ghost. If he's really here, I want to see him."

"I thought you'd like the ghost story," Mrs. Hopkins said. She winked at him. "And I know something about it that no one else does!"

New York,
New York

Fifteen minutes later, Mike, Kate, and Mrs. Hopkins were sitting in the back of a taxi heading to their hotel. It was still a bit chilly outside, but the bright spring sun warmed the car's black vinyl seats.

"Okay, Aunt Laura," Mike said. "Spill it!"

Kate's mom laughed and shook her head. "No way. Reporters don't have info handed to them. You have to learn how to figure it out. But I'll give it to you if you can guess it."

Kate settled back into the seat. This was her type of game. "Is it a person, place, or thing?" she asked.

"Place," her mother replied.

"The locker room!" Mike shouted.

Mrs. Hopkins smiled. "No, Mike, it's not the locker room. You need to ask more general questions until you've narrowed it down. Here's a hint. It's someplace you would like, perhaps around lunchtime."

"Mom, that's giving it away," Kate said with a frown. She didn't like it when puzzles were too simple. She liked figuring things out. "It's either got to be something to do with baseball or food. Is it a food stand?"

"Yes, it is," Mrs. Hopkins said. "Mike?"

"Babe Ruth was famous for eating a lot of hot dogs," Mike said. "So I bet it's a hot dog stand!"

"You got it!" Mrs. Hopkins said. "One of the janitors told me about it. Half an hour before every game, the ghost—or whatever it is—can be heard by Bud's hot dog stand."

"Well, I know where I'm eating breakfast tomorrow!" Mike said.

"Hold on, Mike," Kate's mom said. "We don't need to be at the stadium until four o'clock. Tomorrow we'll sightsee a little. Then we can go to the game early."

"Perfect. There's something I want to show you by Grand Central Station, too," Mike said to Kate.

Back at the hotel, Mike and Kate spent an hour racing each other in the pool. They had contests to see who could hold their breath the longest. Just before dinner, they borrowed Mrs. Hopkins's computer to do research on ghosts. Sitting on the hotel towels in their wet bathing suits, they scrolled through the pages.

"There's not a lot on baseball ghosts," Kate said. "But there's lots of information on regular, everyday ghosts."

She ran a search on the most common signs of ghosts. Usually people heard the sound of footsteps, felt cold air, or smelled strange smells. Sometimes doors or windows opened or closed by themselves. Sometimes objects moved around on their own.

"That's pretty spooky. At least we know what to look for tomorrow," Mike said. "But now I'm hungry! Winning all those swimming races really tired me out."

"You mean watching *me* win all those races, don't you?" Kate said. "Race you to dinner!"

Mike and Kate woke up the next morning when they heard the hotel room door close.

Mrs. Hopkins had just come in with a brown paper bag.

"You should read the article in today's paper," Mrs. Hopkins said. "It's about ghosts." She emptied the bag onto the small round table near the window. Kate's mom had bought a newspaper, some bagels, and orange juice from a nearby store.

Kate opened the newspaper. The first story in the sports section was all about Mr. Robert Williams, his book, and the ghost of Yankee Stadium. Next to the story was a picture of Mr. Williams. He was tall and had a bushy black mustache.

Mike poured a glass of orange juice and read the first few paragraphs of the newspaper story. "See?" he said. "Mr. Williams says that the ghost is real. I'll bet he's hoping the Yankees will hire him to look into it."

Kate helped herself to a bagel. She spread it with butter. "Maybe we should ask *him* about the ghost," she said.

"Don't be so sure he'll help you," Mrs. Hopkins said. "Mr. Williams is a good writer. But he sometimes tells tall tales to help sell his books."

After breakfast, Kate, Mike, and Mrs. Hopkins took a three-hour double-decker bus tour of New York City. Mike and Kate scrambled up to the open-air seats on the top of the bus. They saw the Empire State Building, Rockefeller Center, and Central Park.

Mike was amazed at how big the city was. Tall buildings threw long shadows on the busy streets. Every time the bus turned a corner, Mike leaned over the top railing to look down. The bus was long, and the turns were tight. It always seemed as if the back end would run over a newsstand or trash can.

"I'm glad I'm not a bus driver here," Mike said to Kate. "I'd be worried about smashing into something!"

At the end of the tour, they got off the bus near Grand Central.

"Okay, Mike," Mrs. Hopkins said. She squinted against the afternoon sun. "We're finally at Grand Central. What did you want to show us?"

A steady crowd of workers hustled by them on their way to lunch. Mike studied the nearby buildings. Behind them was a big stone and steel archway to the train station. Right next door were a bank with shiny windows and a few clothing stores.

"It's here somewhere," Mike said. He walked a few feet along the sidewalk toward the bank.

"There it is!" he cried. He pointed at a large skyscraper. "The Grand Hyatt hotel."

Above them, the glass windows of the hotel towered out of sight.

"Oh," Kate said with a yawn. "A big hotel. Like we haven't seen any others today."

"It's not just another hotel, Kate," Mike told her. "It's *the* hotel for baseball. A lot of major-league teams stay here when they come to play. Baseball teams have been staying at this hotel even before it was the Hyatt.

People hang around for autographs. They sometimes catch the players getting on or off the bus before or after games."

Kate looked at the hotel with more interest. "Why didn't you say so?" she asked. "That's kinda cool. Think we'll see anyone?"

"Not if we're going to make it to the game on time ourselves," Mrs. Hopkins said. She checked her watch. "Anyway, the team has probably already left. Now that we've seen the hotel, let's get a snack and find a taxi to the stadium."

"Food! That's a great idea," Mike said. "There's a pretzel cart on the corner."

Mike hurried down the street toward a shiny silver pretzel cart with a bright red umbrella. He was halfway down the block before Kate could reply. "Hey, Mike—wait," she called out.

As she did, there was a loud, rumbling *WHOOSH!* Scraps of paper fluttered up from the sidewalk. Mike's hair blew wildly. He tried to shout something back to Kate, but loud metallic screeching drowned out his voice.

Then the noise was gone.

The papers dropped to the ground.

"What was *that*?" Mike yelled.

"I'd say it was a New York City ghost," Kate said, laughing. "Loud noises, bad smells, papers moving without any reason . . . Did some cool air blow all over you?"

"No, it was hot air. But seriously, Kate, what *was* that?" Mike asked again.

"Well, it *might* have been a ghost. But I think it was just a subway train," Mrs. Hopkins said. "They run right under this street. The screeches were the train's brakes."

"What about all that wind?" Mike asked.

"Look at the sidewalk," Kate said.

Mike looked down. Under his bright red sneakers was a large metal grate. It looked like a big tic-tac-toe board with holes.

"Whenever a subway train comes by, it forces the air in front of it out of the tunnel. The air comes up through those vents," Mrs. Hopkins said. "They're all over the sidewalks here."

"I'm just glad it's not a ghost," Mike said.

At the cart, Mike and Kate got a pretzel to split. "I'm saving room for a hot dog at Bud's," Mike said.

Meanwhile, Mrs. Hopkins hailed a taxi for the ballpark.

"The game starts at four," Mrs. Hopkins said when they reached Yankee Stadium. "It's two o'clock now. You two can check out Bud's hot dog stand if you want. But stay in touch with me so I know where you are."

"No problem, Mom," Kate said. "There aren't any subway grates in Yankee Stadium, so Mike won't get scared."

Mike and Kate waved goodbye to Mrs. Hopkins. They walked along the main corridor. Employees were just opening up food and souvenir stands. They passed a store with rows of dark blue Yankees shirts and hats hanging in front.

"Hey, can we stop at one of these stores?" Kate asked. "I want to get a Yankees shirt before the weekend is over."

"Okay, but let's look for the ghost first," Mike said. "We don't want to miss it."

They passed the food court area. "Remember what we read last night?" Kate asked. They were close to the hot dog stand her mother had told them about. "We're looking for objects that move on their own. And doors and windows opening or closing." She ticked the things off on her fingers. "There might be strange temperatures, funny sounds or smells, or gusts of cool air."

Ahead on their left was the hot dog stand.

For a moment, a white hooded figure poked its head around the side of the stand. Then it vanished.

Mike stopped short. "Did you see that?" he whispered.

"See what?" Kate said. She looked around, confused.

"I don't know." Mike shook his head. He pointed to the hot dog stand. "I thought I saw something over there. It looked like a ghost!"

Kate squinted. All she saw were shadows. "There's nothing there now," she said.

SLAM! A metallic bang echoed through the hallway. Bright light flooded the area. A blast of hot air rushed by. Then it was quiet again. Mike and Kate looked up.

The ghost was right in front of them!

Bud

"Did I scare you?" the ghost asked from behind the counter of the hot dog stand.

"Uh, no," fibbed Kate. "Not really."

"Sorry about that," the ghost said. "The spring on that security grill makes it snap open. I've been asking them to fix that for weeks now. It can be a little surprising if you're not ready for it." He pushed the white hood back over his head. The "ghost" was just a slightly balding older man.

"Name's Bud," he said. "I didn't mean to spook you. Usually there aren't a lot of people around when I open up."

"That was a pretty loud bang," Mike said.

"I know. Sometimes that security grill even scares me." Bud laughed. "How about a free drink to make up for it?"

Mike looked at the row of sodas, juices, and sports drinks on the shelf behind Bud. Blue, red, green, yellow. But he knew what he wanted.

"Thanks!" Mike said. "I'll take a Power-Punch." PowerPunch was his favorite drink.

"Root beer, please," Kate said.

"What brings you two down here so early before a game?" Bud asked as he gave them their drinks.

"Well . . ." Kate paused. He seemed like a nice guy, but she wasn't sure whether they could trust him. She decided to take a chance. Hopefully, he wouldn't laugh at them. "We heard there was a ghost around here and wanted to find it."

Bud smiled. "Ah, the ghost," he said. "You've come to the right place."

Mike elbowed Kate in the ribs.

Bud leaned over the counter. "Of course, I've never *seen* the ghost." His voice dropped to a whisper. "But I've *heard* it. Some of the other employees say they've seen Babe Ruth's ghost walking around the stadium. But I think they're just telling stories. The real ghost is here."

Kate's heart beat faster. This was exactly what she was hoping for. She and Mike leaned closer to catch every word. "When?" Kate asked. "What does it sound like?"

"It's always before a game. I hear Babe

Ruth walking by. It's as if he's right here," Bud said as he patted the counter. "And usually, before I hear the ghost, it gets cold in here."

"Is that why you have the heater?" Kate asked. She pointed to a small heater on the counter.

"Yes," Bud said. "I keep this handy to warm up after the cool breeze."

"How do you know it's a ghost?" asked Mike. "Maybe it's just other noises in the stadium."

"It's got to be a ghost. There's always a quick rush of cool air. Then I hear strange noises. It's like someone walking or scuffling along," Bud said. "I think it's Babe Ruth. He's looking for his locker, but he can't find it in the new stadium."

Mike nodded knowingly. "Strange noises and cold air. Sounds like a ghost to me," he said.

"Is it okay if we look around?" Kate asked.

Bud rubbed a hand across his balding head and glanced at his watch. "Sure," he said. "Make sure you stop back about half an hour before the game. That's when the ghost usually comes."

"Thanks, we will," Kate said.

Mike slipped the half-full bottle of red PowerPunch into his sweatshirt pocket. He nodded at a dark hallway just to the right of the hot dog stand. "What's down there?" he asked.

"That's a service area," Bud said. "Nothing but a couple of storage closets and some trash carts."

Mike and Kate said goodbye and stepped away from the stand. On the left of Bud's was an ice cream counter. On the right was the service hallway. A few early fans walked by.

They seemed to be headed toward the end of the main corridor. Kate could see a smaller passage there.

"I wonder where they're going," she said. Kate and Mike followed the small group of fans into the narrow passageway. Above them were shiny silver pipes snaking back and forth across the ceiling.

Mike dragged his fingers along the white ceramic tile of the wall. The smooth surface felt cool. "Where do you think this goes?" he asked Kate. "It feels like we're in some underground tunnel."

"Probably just around to the first-base side of the stadium," Kate replied. She thought for a minute. "Bud's hot dog stand is near third base. We must be under the seats in center field."

They passed a large white door marked STADIUM OPERATIONS STORAGE ROOM. Just after it on the right side was a small set of stairs leading to a landing.

"Let's check it out," Mike said. He was always up for adventure. He bounded down the stairs and disappeared through a doorway. Half a minute later, he was back, waving to Kate. "Kate—you have to come see this!"

Kate scurried down the stairs and stepped out into bright sunshine. The white walls of the hallway had changed into black granite. A cement sidewalk curved around a small black wall and some large slabs of red rock.

"Wow! What *is* this place?" Kate asked.

"It's Monument Park!" Mike said. "I had forgotten all about it. It's a bunch of monuments to important people from the Yankees. Those three big stones in the center are for Lou Gehrig, Babe Ruth, and a Yankees manager named Miller Huggins."

Kate turned and looked out at the stadium. Rows of seats extended around the ballpark from both sides of Monument Park. Beyond the outfield wall was the red dirt warning track and the green grass outfield. Far across the field was home plate.

"What if they hit a ball here?" she asked. "Is it still a home run?"

"Yup," Mike said. "Since it's over the outfield fence, it's a home run. But it didn't used to be."

"What do you mean?" Kate asked.

"A long time ago, in the original Yankee Stadium, these monuments were in the outfield," Mike said. "Players actually had to chase balls around them."

"It's a good thing they moved them," Kate

said. "I'd hate to smash into one of these if I was chasing down a fly ball."

Kate walked along the curvy path while Mike stayed to read Babe Ruth's monument. She stopped in front of a row of large white circles mounted on the granite wall. Each one had a black number and pinstripes.

"Hey, Mike, these must be the Yankees retired numbers," Kate said. "There's Babe Ruth's number three and Lou Gehrig's number four. This is so cool! You know, back then, players were given a number based on their spot in the batting order."

Mike was about to catch up to Kate when something behind the monuments caught his eye. It was an older man in a Yankees uniform, white with black pinstripes. At first Mike thought it was one of the Yankees players stopping by before the game. But then he noticed how old and worn the uniform looked.

The man stared right past Mike, to the Yankees dugout. Without a word, he tipped his baseball hat toward the field. Then he moved past the monuments and disappeared up the stairs.

Mike shook his head and hurried over to Kate. "Did you see that?" he asked her.

"See what?" Kate asked. She was standing in front of the big brass plaque dedicated to Lou Gehrig. "Did you know Lou Gehrig was one of the best Yankees hitters of all time?"

"Yes, but I'm talking about the guy who was just here," Mike said. "He was wearing an old-fashioned Yankees uniform."

"It was probably just a fan," Kate said. She flipped her ponytail. "Or maybe someone who works at one of the stores."

"I don't know," Mike said. "There was

something strange about him. We should be on the lookout for him."

"Monument Park will be closing shortly," a security guard near the doorway called out. "We close forty-five minutes before every game. Please feel free to come back before the next game."

"Hey, that means we have to go listen for the ghost soon!" Kate said.

"Race you there," Mike said. He took off running. Kate bounded up the stairs and followed him.

Just before Bud's, Mike turned right down the service hallway. When Kate turned the corner, he was gone.

The only thing Kate saw in the long hallway was a large black trash cart at the far end.

"Mike?" she called.

At the end of the hallway were two steel

doors. *They must be the storage closets that Bud mentioned,* Kate thought.

She walked to the hallway's end and tried to decide which door to open. Mike could be hiding in either one. She picked the door on the left.

Kate took a breath and reached for the handle.

But before she touched it, the handle turned and the door swung open all by itself.

Cool Air and Noises

"Umph!" Kate said as she ran into a large brown box. She looked up. She had actually hit a man *carrying* a large brown box.

"Whoa!" The man steadied himself and stepped back. "I'm sorry. I didn't expect anyone to be here. Are you okay?"

"Yes, thanks. I'm fine," Kate said. The man was tall and had a black mustache. The large cardboard box in his hands was labeled BOOKS. "Hey, you're Mr. Williams!"

The man smiled. His bushy black mustache pulled up high on the sides. It made his face look extra wide.

"The one and only. Pleased to meet you," Mr. Williams said. With a grunt, he placed the box of books on the floor.

"I'm Kate Hopkins," she said. "We just read about you in the newspaper this morning. You're an expert on ghosts in ballparks!"

"We?" Mr. Williams said.

"Me and Kate," Mike said. He stepped forward from somewhere behind Kate. "I'm Mike, Kate's cousin."

Kate looked suspiciously at Mike. A quick glance showed her that the hallway was still empty except for the large trash cart. That was probably where he had been hiding.

"We heard there's a ghost around here," Mike went on.

Mr. Williams shifted his weight from one leg to the other. He smoothed his mustache with his thumb and first finger. "Well, yes, I've heard that, too," he said after a minute. "Maybe you two would like to stop by later and buy a copy of my book on baseball ghosts. I'll be signing them near gate four."

"Oh, maybe," Mike said. "Do you think this ghost is real? We know someone who's heard it."

"It's the ghost of Babe Ruth," added Kate. "He's making strange noises."

"It might be. But even if it is, I'm afraid it's not something for children to poke their noses into," Mr. Williams said. "Real ghosts can be scary. You never know what's going to happen. It's probably best to stay away and just enjoy today's game."

Mr. Williams's cell phone beeped. He pulled

it out of his pocket and looked at the screen.

"I'm sorry. I'm late for a meeting," Mr. Williams said. He slipped the phone back into his pocket and bent down to pick up the box of books. "Please, buy my book if you're interested in ghosts. But don't go looking for them. You might end up in trouble."

Mr. Williams walked away into the rush of people in the main corridor. It was close to game time, and the stadium was filling up with fans.

"I'll bet he doesn't want us looking around because there is no ghost. It's just Mr. Williams spreading rumors. It's all to help sell his books," Mike said. "Like your mom said."

"I don't think that's it. Remember, Bud told us that he's heard the ghost himself a bunch of times," Kate said. "He wouldn't say that unless he did hear it, or unless Mr. Williams is paying him to say it. But Bud seems like too nice a guy to lie like that."

"We should get back to Bud's," Mike said. He pulled Kate toward the hot dog stand. "The ghost usually comes about now."

"So where were you going when I was chasing you?" Kate asked as they walked along.

"I wanted to get back at you for sneaking up on me yesterday after the press conference," Mike said. "I was going to jump out and scare you. But Williams got you first!"

In the main corridor, fans were streaming by, trying to reach their seats in time. Mike and Kate stopped in front of Bud's.

"Hey, it's the ghost detectives," Bud said, taking a break from filling popcorn buckets. "If you're so smart, maybe you can answer a question. What do ghosts serve for dessert?"

"Wait—I know this one," Kate said. "Boo-berries?"

Bud smiled. "Nope, but nice try," he said. "How about you, Mike?"

"I don't know," Mike said. "What do ghosts serve for dessert?"

"Ice *scream*!" Bud slapped the counter and laughed. "So, what can I get you two?"

They bought two hot dogs each. Kate put mustard and relish on hers. Mike loaded his up with ketchup and pulled the bottle of red PowerPunch from his sweatshirt pocket.

Mike bit into his hot dog and took a gulp of PowerPunch. In between bites, he stopped and listened for the ghost. But all he could hear was the rustle of the crowd. In the background, the ballpark announcer called out the starting lineup.

"It's getting near game time. Maybe the ghost isn't coming tonight," Mike said to Kate. "Let's go to our seats. We can wait for it tomorrow instead."

"Just hang on a minute more," Kate begged.

They watched a customer order popcorn and a soda.

"Some nights it's popcorn. Some nights it's hot dogs," Bud said as the woman walked away. "You never can tell." He mopped his brow.

There was a rush of cool air. Kate and Mike felt the hair on their arms tingle.

"Here it comes," Bud said. "The ghost of Babe Ruth is in the house!"

KRRRRTT. SWWWWSSSSH. KRRRRTT.

Above them—or somewhere behind the stand—they heard muffled scraping and rustling sounds. For a minute or two, the sounds got louder, and then they got softer.

"That didn't sound like Babe Ruth walking by," Mike said. "It sounded more like Babe Ruth with a broken leg dragging his bat and a duffel bag across the roof of a car."

Bud nodded. "Well, it sounds a little bit different each time. But that's the ghost."

"Let's go see if we can find it," Kate said. She tossed her napkin in the trash. "Thanks for the help, Bud!"

"No problem," Bud said. "Good luck. If you find Babe, get me an autograph!"

By the edge of the hot dog stand, Mike and Kate peered around the corner into the low light of the service hallway.

"It sounded like that noise came from down there!" Kate said. Her forehead wrinkled. "I don't see anything except those storage closets at the end of the hallway."

"We never got a good look inside them," Mike pointed out. "Maybe we can find a clue to the ghost if we check them out."

Kate nodded, and they tiptoed down the hallway to the end.

Mike pulled open the large metal door on the right. Inside stood a broom, a dustpan, and a mop.

"It's just a closet. No ghost," Mike said. "Try the other one."

Kate was about to turn the handle when they heard voices on the other side of the door. With a small creak, it cracked open an inch.

Kate took a quick step back. There was no time for them to hide!

A second later, the door swept open. The bottom edge missed hitting Kate's foot by inches.

Three people popped out of the room. The door slammed shut.

Kate and Mike stood still. Maybe in the darkness, the people wouldn't see them. The three figures started walking down the hallway.

Mike relaxed. He leaned against the wall. As he did, his baseball slid out of the front pocket of his sweatshirt. It dropped to the ground.

CLUNK!

Mike froze. Shocked, Kate stared at the baseball lying on the floor. They were busted!

The three figures stopped. They spun around.

"Hey, it's Mickey Mantle," said the first

person. "What are you doing here? This area is for employees only."

Mike knew the voice right away. It was Sammy, the redheaded teenager he had met the day before. Sammy still had his Yankees cap on. But instead of the blue ACE AIR-CONDITIONING shirt, he was wearing a pin-striped Yankees replica jersey. In his left hand, he carried a small flashlight.

"Uh, we were just looking around," Kate said from over Mike's shoulder.

"Well, there's nothing here except store-rooms," Sammy said. He looked at Kate sus-piciously. "We were putting some stuff away for my father's air-conditioning company."

Sammy's two friends shrugged and contin-ued down the hall. "We're going to find seats, Sammy," the shorter boy said. "Meet us in the usual place—section two-twenty-six."

"You two probably shouldn't be here," Sammy said to Kate and Mike. "You might get in trouble."

"Uh, okay, thanks," Mike said. He picked up the baseball and tucked it back into his pocket. Then he gave Kate's arm a tug. "Come on."

Sammy watched them leave.

Mike and Kate turned the corner.

"Who was that? How do you know him?" Kate asked. "And why did he call you Mickey Mantle?"

"That's Sammy. I saw him yesterday after the press conference, when you were getting Aunt Laura," Mike said. "I dropped my baseball. He picked it up and threw it back to me. He was calling me Mickey Mantle just to give me a hard time."

"What's he doing here?" Kate asked. "Do

you think he has something to do with Mr. Williams?"

"I don't know," Mike said. He looked over his shoulder to see if Sammy was around. There was no sign of him or his friends. "It's probably not safe to go in there now, in case he comes back. But I really want to see what's in that room. I have a feeling it's the key to Babe Ruth's ghost!"

Seventh-Inning
Stretch

By now, it was getting dark outside. But the stadium's bright lights lit up the field as if it were noon. It was a perfect, cool spring night for a baseball game, but not for the Seattle Mariners. After three innings, the Yankees were ahead by two runs. And after six innings, they were beating the Mariners by five.

Halfway through the next inning came the seventh-inning stretch. The grounds crew hustled out to rake the baselines. The fans stood up to stretch. The organ music for "Take Me Out to the Ball Game" started. As soon as people began to sing along, Mike and Kate left their seats. Mike figured it was a good time to check out the storage room.

The food area was filling up with fans. In the background, the stadium's organ played. Mike and Kate could hear the fans singing, *"Take me out to the ball game. Take me out with the crowd. . . ."*

"Hurry!" Mike said. The only thing in the service hallway was still the black trash cart.

When they got to the doors at the end, Kate gave a quick glance back toward Bud's. "No one is watching," she said.

Mike turned the knob and gave the door a push. It didn't budge. He pushed harder, but the door didn't move.

Kate checked again. The coast was still clear. "Let me try it," she said. She turned the knob in the other direction and pushed. It wouldn't move.

"How about pulling it?" Mike asked.

Kate smiled and pulled on the door. It swung open easily. The room was dark. "Yup, pull instead of push," she said. "I should have remembered that."

"All right!" Mike whispered. "You go first!"

Kate tiptoed in.

"Hit the light switch," Mike said.

Kate fumbled along the wall with her right hand. No light switch. All she could feel was a metal shelf. "It's got to be here," she said. She tried a little bit lower. Finally, her hand found a switch. She flipped it up.

The room was empty except for an old chair and a pile of cardboard boxes against the back wall. A small light hung from the ceiling. A set of metal shelves stood to the left of the door in front of the light switch.

"Nothing here but some boxes," Mike said. He walked over to the pile and peeked inside the top box. "I think we've found a ghost!"

Kate rushed over.

Inside the box was Mr. Williams's book on baseball ghosts.

Kate smirked. "Ha-ha," she said.

They searched the room for other clues. Something on the floor caught Kate's eye. She bent over. "Mike, take a look at this," she said.

Small specks of brown littered the chair and the floor. There was a thin trail of it leading from the chair to the door. Kate picked up a pinch and smelled it.

"What is it?" asked Mike.

"Dirt," she said. "And something that

looks like wood chips. But what's dirt doing here?"

"I don't know . . . ," Mike said. "Hmmm . . . let's think. Maybe because it's a ballpark and the whole field is made of dirt and grass?"

Kate crossed her arms. "I think it's a clue," she said.

"Someone forgot to wipe their feet," Mike said. "My mom's always yelling at me about that. Maybe real baseball players have the same problem."

Kate shook her head. She pointed to the wall behind the chair. There was a line of small scratches and scuffs in the gray paint of the wall below a vent. "What about these scratches?" she asked. "What are they from?"

Mike leaned in and studied the marks. "Maybe someone was trying to scratch their way out!"

Kate rolled her eyes. "Get real! Stop joking around!"

"Okay, okay," Mike said. "They don't look like much to me. I'll bet someone was just using this room to change his shoes or store equipment or something." He shrugged. "Let's go. There's nothing else here."

Mike took a sip of his PowerPunch and slid the bottle back into his sweatshirt pocket. At the same time, he pulled out his baseball and started tossing it in the air.

"Can't you ever stop tossing that baseball?" asked Kate.

"It helps me think," Mike said. He looked over at Kate and made a face. But as he did, the ball went flying out of his hand.

It sailed toward the back wall.

"Uh-oh!" Mike cried. He covered his eyes with his hands.

SLAM!

The ball clanged against the air vent cover in the back wall. It dropped with a clunk onto the concrete floor.

Mike was afraid to look. It wouldn't be the

first time he had broken something with a baseball.

"You can open your eyes now," Kate said. Mike did. Kate was frowning at him. "Hopefully, no one heard that," she went on. "Sammy is right. You *do* need to work on your catching."

Mike picked up his ball. It seemed okay. "Well, at least it didn't do any damage," he said.

"Um, maybe not to the ball, knucklehead, but what about that?" Kate asked.

She pointed to the corner of the air vent, where the ball had hit it. The bottom edge of the large square metal grate stuck out from the wall.

"Oops," Mike said. He leaned in. Luckily, the ball hadn't dented the grate. It had just knocked it loose. He started to push it back in, but Kate stopped him.

"Wait! I have an idea," she said.

Kate moved Mike aside. She stood in front of the air vent and grabbed its lower corners. She wiggled the bottom edge away from the wall. With a snap, it swung open. "Ta-da!" she said. "Pretty good, eh?"

"Wow, how'd you do that?" Mike asked.

"When you were pushing on the grate, I noticed the hinge along the top," Kate said. "So I figured it would swing up for cleaning."

Mike pushed the chair under the vent while Kate held it open. Then they both hopped up on the chair to have a look. As they did, the bottle of PowerPunch in Mike's sweatshirt pocket banged against the wall.

"Shh!" Kate warned. "Are you trying to get us caught?"

Mike shook his head and slipped the bottle out of his pocket. He took another quick sip. Then he set the bottle down in the big metal vent.

"It's an air vent," Kate said. "Like the ones in my house, only a lot bigger."

"How do you know?" asked Mike. He stood on his tippy-toes to get a better look.

"My father showed me how our furnace works when we were cleaning our basement last fall," Kate said. "I'll bet this is an air return. Air returns bring air back to a furnace or air conditioner."

"This is a pretty big vent," Mike said.

"Hey, look at that," Kate said. She pointed to small clumps of dirt and slivers of brown wood chips on the inside of the vent.

"Wow—just like on the chair and the floor!" Mike said. He reached out and picked up one of the brown clumps. It smelled like his mother's garden. It was definitely dirt.

"Yeah. Something funny is going on," Kate said. "Let's get out of here. Watch out while I close this."

Mike stepped back, but he'd forgotten he was standing on the chair. For a second, he lost his balance. He tried to steady himself, but his right arm knocked into his half-full bottle of PowerPunch. The bottle wobbled. It tipped over. The red liquid spilled into the vent, leaving a large puddle.

"Oh no!" Kate said. "Nice job, Mr. Clean!"

Mike turned as red as the PowerPunch. He could be really clumsy sometimes.

Kate sighed. "Stand here and hold the cover open. I'll look for something to mop it up with," she said.

She hopped off the chair and scanned the room. There was nothing except the empty shelves and Mr. Williams's books.

Suddenly, the kids heard a loud crash out-side the door.

"Hurry up, Kate!" Mike whispered.

Kate looked at the small pool of Power-Punch. "It won't hurt anything to leave it," she whispered back. "There's not that much. It will dry up in a day or two. Quick, grab the bottle and help me close this."

Ten seconds later, Mike and Kate had the vent cover back on. They peeked out of the door into the service hallway.

"There's no one here. That noise must have just been someone throwing a bag of trash into the cart," Kate said. "Let's get out of here before anyone else comes."

The Troublemakers

Kate and Mike hurried down the service hall-way and back to the main corridor.

"Hey, kids!"

Someone had seen them leaving the store-room!

"Over here!"

They turned around. It was Bud, waving them over to his hot dog stand.

"I'm glad I caught you," he said. "I just thought of something. What do you say when you meet a ghost?"

Before either one of them could answer, Bud pounded the counter. "How do you *boo*?" he said. "Get it? How do you *boo*?"

Kate rolled her eyes. "Thanks, Bud," she said. "That's good. Have you heard the ghost lately?"

"No," Bud said. "But I just remembered I have a message for you. From the ghost."

Kate raised her eyebrows. "You do?" she asked. "From the ghost?"

"Well, no, not really. But it is from the ghost *expert*," Bud replied. "Mr. Williams stopped by. He knew you two were looking around earlier. He wanted me to tell you that ghost hunting isn't for kids. But if you stop by his autograph table, he'll have something special for you."

Mike tugged on Kate's sleeve. "Thanks for the message, Bud. Maybe we'll see you later," he said.

"Okay," Bud said. "Come back after the game if you want a hot dog!"

"Mr. Williams must have seen us sneaking into the room," Mike said when they were out of earshot of Bud. "What should we do?"

"No, he didn't," Kate said, shaking her head. "He's talking about when I bumped into him before the game. I'll bet he's just trying to scare us off the trail."

"You mean scare us off *his* trail," Mike said. "He was in the storeroom just before we heard the ghost. Maybe he put something in that vent to make noise or blow cold air. Nobody would suspect him because he's storing his books back there."

Kate nodded. "We should stake out that storeroom tomorrow and see if it happens again."

Kate and Mike were soon back in their

seats near third base. It was the top of the ninth inning. There were no outs yet. Seattle had just scored two runs, but the Yankees were still ahead, five to two.

With his first swing, one of Seattle's best batters hit a high foul ball down the first-base line. On the next pitch, he hit another high-flying foul ball. This one soared back toward Mike's and Kate's seats.

Mike jumped up. "I've got it! I've got it!" he yelled. He stretched to catch the ball.

The ball sailed right over him.

"Bummer," Mike said.

In the next section over, a little boy in a Yankees uniform tried to catch the ball in his small glove. A redheaded teenager snagged the ball instead. He held the ball up. The fans around him clapped and whistled.

Then the redhead turned and gave the

little boy the baseball he had caught. The boy waved the baseball around just like the teenager had. The nearby fans all cheered for him.

"Isn't that Sammy, the guy who called you Mickey Mantle?" Kate asked. She pointed to the red-haired teenager.

Mike nodded. "Yup, that's Sammy," he said. "But he's a dummy. If I caught a ball, I'd keep it. It's probably worth seventy-five dollars."

"Aw, I think it was nice of him," Kate said. "That little kid is really happy and—"

Suddenly, Mike waved his hand to quiet her. "Shh . . . ," he said. He leaned toward the aisle. He was trying to listen to an usher. She was talking to a fan on the other side of the aisle. Kate listened, too.

"So, like I said, be careful!" the usher told a fan in a striped shirt. "Babe Ruth's ghost is haunting the stadium!"

The usher started to head down the stairs. But Mike waved to her. She stopped next to them.

"We just heard you talking about a ghost," Mike said. "Have you seen the one at Bud's hot dog stand?"

"I know that Bud has been telling people about it," the usher said. "But I think it's just a scary story he made up. That's not the real ghost at all."

"Oh," Kate said. "It sounded kinda real to us."

The usher leaned forward. "Can you keep a secret?"

Mike and Kate nodded.

"Like I was just telling that other fan, the real ghost is the ghost of Babe Ruth. He's walking around the stadium," the usher said. "I've seen him in an old-fashioned pin-striped uniform before games. Sometimes he's in the stands. Once he was in the dugout. But he vanishes every time I try to get a good look at him."

Mike sucked his breath in. Kate was about to ask another question, but the usher took a step away from them.

"I'm sorry. You'll have to excuse me," she said, looking back over her shoulder. "I see a couple of troublemakers over in section two-twenty-six. They're always trying to sit in someone else's seats."

When the usher left, Kate grabbed Mike's arm, her eyes wide. "Wow!" she said. "That sounds like the guy you saw in Monument Park! Maybe it's the same ghost that's haunting Bud's hot dog stand!"

The usher had reached section 226. To Mike's surprise, she went right over to Sammy and his friends. She spoke to them. Then Sammy rummaged through his pockets. He held out his empty hands. The usher motioned for him and his friends to leave the seats.

Sammy and his friends headed into the stands. The usher watched them go. Then she turned around to help other fans.

"Did you see that?" Mike asked Kate. "Sammy—"

Just then, the crowd roared to life. All around Mike and Kate, fans stood up and started clapping.

Mike checked the scoreboard. It was still the top of the ninth inning. The Mariners had two outs now, but they had runners on all the bases. The count was three balls, two strikes. One more strike and the game would be over. But a home run would score four runs and put the Mariners one ahead. Then the Yankees would have just one more turn at bat.

The Yankees pitcher put his head down. He stared at the catcher. He shook off one sign after another. The fans clapped louder. They wanted that last out! Finally, the pitcher got a call he liked. He stood up straight, cupped the ball in his glove, reeled back, and let the ball fly.

The Mariners batter swung hard. The bat slammed into the ball.

The clapping stopped. The stadium was quiet. The ball flew high into center field. The fans groaned. One after the other, the Mariners base runners scored. The ball

plummeted into Monument Park. The batter crossed home plate.

It was a grand slam! Four runs for Seattle! The Yankees fans slumped into their seats. Now they needed at least one run to tie the game. Otherwise, they would lose.

Luckily for the Yankees, the next Seattle batter popped out. The Yankees had one more chance to tie the game or get ahead.

But they weren't able to. Three strikeouts later, the game was over. Seattle had won.

Mike shook his head sadly as they got up to leave. "They were *soooo* close!" he said. "If only that Seattle batter hadn't hit a grand slam."

"I know," Kate said. "There's always tomorrow's game. And if we hurry, we can stop by the souvenir stand to buy a shirt before we meet my mother."

A few minutes later, they were standing in line at the souvenir shop near the food court. Kate had a dark blue New York Yankees shirt in her hand.

WHOOSH! The air vent above them came on full blast. A rush of cool air blew through the shop.

Mike jumped. "Wow, that's cold," he said. "Maybe you should buy a Yankees jacket instead of a shirt! Those vents come on fast."

Kate grabbed Mike's arm. "That's it! The air conditioner vent!" she said. "It's just like the subway grates on the sidewalk. Remember how the subway train pushed all that air up through the sidewalk vents?"

"Yes, so it looked funny when I jumped a little bit," Mike said. "But it was a whole lot funnier when you dropped that package of eggs at my house because my father scared you."

"You're missing the point, Mike," Kate said. "The ghostly chill. Remember? What if the cold air in the air-conditioning vent near Bud's hot dog stand got pushed out all at once? It would be just the same as when the subway train went by!"

"It would feel like a ghost!" Mike said.

"But why would that happen? Do you think the subway next to the stadium is doing it somehow?"

"No, but what if the other end of that vent was outside? It's still spring, so it's colder outside the stadium," Kate said. "Maybe someone opened up the other end of the vent. That would let in a rush of cold air all at once, like a ghost!"

"So that's why Bud always feels the chill and *then* hears the noise," Mike said. "But who is opening the air-conditioning vent?"

"I'm not sure. But there's one way to find out," Kate said. "Let's get here early before tomorrow's game. I think I know how to solve the mystery!"

The Red Stain

In the morning, Kate and Mike could hardly wait to get to the ballpark. They sat impatiently through a late breakfast. They fidgeted while Mrs. Hopkins talked to her boss on the phone. Finally, they left the hotel. The game started at one o'clock.

When they got to the ballpark it was noon. Kate was nervous. What if they missed their chance?

"I'll see you later," Mrs. Hopkins said.

"Enjoy the game. If you need me, I'll be in the pressroom." She turned and walked to the elevator.

"Mike, hurry!" Kate said. "Race you to the hot dog stand!"

She tagged Mike and took off. They tore down the stairs and past crowds of fans going to their seats. Kate touched the counter of the hot dog stand seconds before her cousin.

"Beat you," Kate panted.

"No fair," Mike said. "You had a head start." He bent over to catch his breath. "I'm thirsty. Wait up while I get a PowerPunch."

A long line of customers snaked back from the stand. Bud was working quickly to keep up with the orders for hot dogs, pretzels, and sodas.

"Skip the drink," Kate said to Mike. "There's no time to waste."

"Okay," Mike said. "But you owe me one."

They slipped past the customers and into the service hallway. Near the end, Mike and Kate crouched behind the large black trash cart. No one could see them there. And it gave them a perfect view of the storeroom.

But after fifteen minutes, Mike started rubbing his legs. "I'm getting sore," he said. "Can we stand up for a minute?"

"No, we need to stay hidden," whispered Kate. "It's a good thing you're not a catcher. You wouldn't last more than a few batters!"

Kate peeked around the edge of the trash cart. Suddenly, she grabbed Mike's arm. "It's him! It's him! Here comes Mr. Williams," she hissed.

Mr. Williams was walking toward them with big strides. His eyes darted from side to side.

"He saw us!" Mike whispered. "What do we do now?"

"Shh!" Kate said. "He didn't see us."

Just before the storage room, Mr. Williams stopped and looked around. He opened the metal door and stepped inside.

"I knew he had something to do with this!" Mike cried.

"Shh!" Kate said again.

A few minutes passed. Then the door swung open. Mr. Williams came out of the storage room carrying a large brown cardboard box. The side of the box read BOOKS. He continued down the hall.

Mike sighed and slumped against the wall. "He's just getting his books," he said.

"The books are his cover," Kate answered. "I'll bet he goes in there and opens that vent. Then he sets something up to make that noise after he leaves. Maybe he calls someone to open the vent outside and let in cold air. It's the perfect excuse!"

A few more minutes ticked by. The crowd near the hot dog stand thinned out.

"Do you think the ghost is going to show up today?" asked Mike. "It's getting close to game time."

"He'll be here," Kate said.

They waited and watched. Kate checked the time.

"This is boring," Mike groaned. He fidgeted with his baseball.

Just then, they heard the ghostly sound. It came from right near them!

KRRRRTT. SWWWWSSSSH. KRRRRTT.

"Babe Ruth's ghost!" Mike whispered.

"Shh," Kate hushed him a third time. The sound ended. "Now, let's see if Mr. Williams comes back. He'll need to undo whatever made the ghostly sounds."

Nothing more happened. No sounds. No Mr. Williams. Maybe their theory wasn't right.

"He's not coming, Kate," Mike said.

Mike was about to stand up when the door to the storeroom cracked open. After a few seconds, Sammy and his friends came out.

Sammy was wearing the same Yankees

pin-striped jersey from the day before. But the bottom front edge was stained a bright cherry red. Behind them, the door slammed shut. Sammy and his friends joined the crowd in the main hallway.

Mike laughed. "I guess I'm not the only clumsy one around!" he said. "Sammy spilled something all over his jersey."

Kate jumped up. "Mike—that's it! The PowerPunch!"

"The PowerPunch?" Mike asked. "What's PowerPunch got to do with anything?"

"Not just any PowerPunch," Kate said. "*Your* PowerPunch! Remember when you spilled it in the vent yesterday?"

"Yeah, so what?" Mike asked.

Kate stamped her foot. "Don't you see?" she said. She got frustrated when her cousin didn't keep up with her thinking. "*You* spilled the PowerPunch in the vent yesterday. I'll bet some of it was still there today, since we didn't clean it up. I'll bet the red stain on Sammy's shirt came from your spilled Power-Punch!"

"You think he crawled through the vent? And his shirt dragged through the Power-Punch?" asked Mike. "Why would Sammy be climbing through the vent?"

"Because he and his friends are sneaking into the stadium!" Kate said. "It all fits. It's *not* Mr. Williams! The air-conditioning duct must start somewhere outside the stadium. Probably near a flower bed or park. That's why we saw the dirt and wood chips on the floor of the storeroom. It came from their sneakers!"

"That means the ghost sounds that we heard were actually Sammy and his friends crawling through the ducts," Mike said.

"Yes," Kate said. "Sammy and his friends are the ghosts!"

Babe Ruth's Ghost

Kate sprang up and pulled the door to the storeroom open. She clicked on the light. The room was empty.

"Hey, look at that," Mike said. He pointed to the fresh bits of dirt leading from the back wall to the door.

"What are you kids doing in here?" asked a deep voice.

Mike and Kate whirled around. "Mr. Williams!" they said.

"Didn't I tell you two to leave the ghosts to me?" Mr. Williams asked.

"But . . . ," Mike started. "We were—"

"Never mind," Mr. Williams said. "I've been looking for you."

"You have?" Mike asked. "Why?"

"Bud told me you were still hunting for ghosts," Mr. Williams said. He frowned. His eyebrows drew together in a dark line.

"Yes, we were," Kate said. "But we just figured out who the ghost is!"

Mr. Williams's eyes opened wide. "You did?" he asked.

Kate explained quickly what they had seen.

Mr. Williams rubbed his mustache. "Of course!" he said. "That's why the ghost stories here were confusing. This is important information you've found out. We should tell security."

Mike looked at his feet. "I don't want to get Sammy in trouble," he said. "But I guess you're right."

Mr. Williams led them to the stadium's security office. There, for the second time, Mike and Kate explained the mystery of the ghost.

"You two are real ghost hunters," the security chief said. "But we'll take it from here. Why don't you go enjoy the game? I'll meet you in the pressroom afterward and give you an update."

Mike and Kate went to their seats. The Yankees were behind by two runs. With all the excitement, the cousins found it hard to concentrate on the game. But they cheered along with the other fans when the Yankees hit three home runs to come back and win.

After the game ended, Mike and Kate went to the pressroom. The security chief was there with Kate's mom, Bud, and Mr. Williams. Most of the reporters and photographers had already left. Mike and Kate sat down in two dark blue chairs near the front windows.

"What happened?" asked Mike.

"After you told us about the ghost, our ushers found Sammy and his friends," the chief said. "We brought them to the security office and called their parents. They admitted to sneaking into Yankee Stadium through the air vent."

Mike swiveled around in his chair and nodded at Kate.

"I knew it," Kate said. "Once I saw Sammy with the punch on his shirt, I knew it had to be him."

"How were they getting into the vent?" Mr. Williams asked. "Aren't the vents usually covered?"

The chief held up a small, shiny gold object. Kate leaned forward to get a good look at it.

"Sammy's father has keys to all of our air-conditioning systems," the chief said. "Sammy took this one. He used it to unlock a special access closet on the outside of the stadium. It's right behind the bushes near the parking garage. The boys climbed into the vent there. We're going to give it back to his father."

"That's where the dirt and wood chips were coming from," Mike said.

Just as Mike and Kate had figured out, the ghostly events were caused by Sammy. The chief said that since it was spring, the air-conditioning wasn't on yet, so Sammy wasn't in any danger. But when he opened the out-side vent cover, the cold spring air came rush-ing in all at once.

"Like this?" Mike asked. He spun his chair around and reached for the handle of one of the big pressroom windows. With a small nudge, he slid the window open. A rush of cool air blew into the room. It swept stray scraps of paper from the nearby desks.

"Mike! You'd better shut that window," Mrs. Hopkins said. "Look at the mess you're making!"

"That's exactly what the ghost felt like!" Bud said.

Mike and Kate laughed. Mike closed the window and took one last look at the stadium. On the field, men and woman in blue shirts were raking the infield dirt and removing the white bases. He swiveled back to face the room.

"Sammy seemed nice," Kate said. "He even gave away that ball he caught. It's too bad he was sneaking in without paying."

"He is a good kid," the chief said. "He's been working here with his dad, and people like him a lot. But he made a bad decision about using the key to sneak in."

"Why didn't he just buy tickets?" Mrs. Hopkins asked.

"He loves the Yankees, but didn't want to spend money on tickets. He's trying to save for college," the chief said. "He was working with his father during school vacations and the summer to earn extra money."

"Are you going to arrest him and his friends?" Mike asked.

"No. But they are going to have to pay us back for all the games they sneaked into," the chief said. "Sammy has already agreed to work on Saturdays until the tickets are paid off. He'll help out around the stadium."

The security chief rustled around in his front pocket and pulled out two shiny white strips of paper with gold writing on them. They looked like some type of special ticket.

"I wanted to thank you for solving our ghostly mystery," he said. He handed a white-and-gold ticket to Mike and Kate. "Without your help, the stadium would still be haunted! Next time you're here, let me know. You can use these special passes to see the game from the owner's box."

Mike and Kate turned the tickets over in their hands. The front of the tickets had a special hologram image of Yankee Stadium and the words OWNER'S PASS written in bright gold letters. The back of each ticket was stamped VALID FOR ANY GAME.

"Wow! That would be great," Mike said. "Does that mean we can tell the manager who to put in the game?"

The security chief laughed. "No, I don't think so. I'm afraid not even our owner can do that. But you could say hello to the manager instead."

Mike smiled. "I've never watched a game from a luxury box before," he said.

"Oh, I almost forgot," Mr. Williams said. "I was looking for you earlier because I had something for you."

He reached into a bag and pulled out two copies of *Ghosts in the Ballpark*. He handed one each to Kate and Mike. "But maybe you don't need any advice on ballpark ghosts anymore," he said. "You two seem to be doing pretty well on your own."

"Thanks," Kate said. "But I do have a question. One of the ushers told us she's seen a strange man dressed in pinstripes around the stadium before games. Whenever she goes over to get a better look, he's gone."

"I think I saw him before yesterday's game," Mike said. "He was in Monument Park. He tipped his hat toward the field and then disappeared up the stairs."

"I haven't heard about that one," Mr.

Williams said. "Maybe we have another ghost on the loose!"

"At first we thought it was the same ghost that Bud was talking about," Mike said. "But it can't be Sammy, because he's outside the stadium before the games. Who do you think it is?"

"Well, I don't know for sure," Mr. Williams said. He tugged on his mustache. "Maybe it's the *real* ghost of Babe Ruth!"

Dugout Notes
☆ Yankee Stadium ☆

"The House That Ruth Built." The Yankees bought Babe Ruth's contract from the Boston Red Sox in 1919. Back then, the Yankees didn't have their own home park. Instead, they played at the Polo Grounds. But the Yankees' rivals, the New York Giants, owned the Polo Grounds.

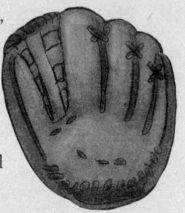

Starting in 1920, huge crowds came to see Babe Ruth hit home runs for the Yankees. The Yankees became more popular than the Giants. That made the Giants' owner mad. In 1921, he told the Yankees to leave. Two years later, Yankee Stadium opened.

Babe Ruth, Hot Dogs, and Horsing Around. Babe Ruth liked to set baseball records. He set a career home run record (714) that wasn't broken until Hank Aaron hit number 715 in 1974. But Ruth also liked to break the rules. Many times he acted like a kid. He was often more interested in having fun than in doing what he was supposed to do. Sometimes Ruth wore the same underwear for days because he didn't feel like changing it. He claimed he could burp louder than a tractor, and he liked to prove it to anyone who would listen. Ruth also ate and drank too much. His midnight meals were larger than most people's dinners. He would eat six hot dogs and drink six sodas for a snack!

A First. Yankee Stadium was the first baseball park to be called a stadium. It was much larger than other ballparks. Yankee Stadium often had crowds of 70,000 people or more. It opened on April 18, 1923. On opening day, the Yankees played the Boston Red Sox. They beat them 4–1. The stadium was also the first triple-decker. That meant it had three seating levels.

Secret Room. The original Yankee Stadium had a secret. For years, there was a fifteen-foot-wide room hidden below second base. The room wasn't used for baseball or storing treasure. It was used for boxing. Yankee Stadium used to host boxing matches sometimes. The hidden room held the electrical and telephone equipment needed for the matches. The Yankees removed the room in 1976. It doesn't exist in the new Yankee Stadium.

Lots of World Series. Yankee Stadium has hosted more World Series than any other stadium—over thirty-five so far.

New and Improved. When it was built in 1923, Yankee Stadium was the best stadium around. But by the early twenty-first century, it was getting old. The team decided it needed a new home. So it spent over $1.3 billion to build a brand-new version of Yankee Stadium directly across the street. The first official game in the new stadium was on April 16, 2009.

The following year, the old stadium was torn down and the land was turned into a park.

Pinstripes. The New York Yankees uniforms are famous for the thin black stripes running up and down the pants and shirts. The Yankees first wore pinstripes in 1912.

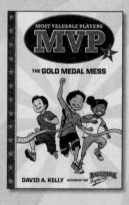
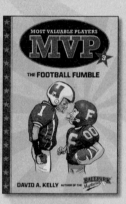